Francis Robert Raines

The Easter rolls of Whalley in the years 1552 and 1553

From the originals at Stonyhurst

Francis Robert Raines

The Easter rolls of Whalley in the years 1552 and 1553
From the originals at Stonyhurst

ISBN/EAN: 9783741190780

Manufactured in Europe, USA, Canada, Australia, Japa

Cover: Foto ©Andreas Hilbeck / pixelio.de

Manufactured and distributed by brebook publishing software
(www.brebook.com)

Francis Robert Raines

The Easter rolls of Whalley in the years 1552 and 1553

THE

Easter Rolls of Whalley

IN THE YEARS

1552 AND 1553.

FROM THE ORIGINALS AT STONYHURST.

EDITED BY

THE REV. CANON RAINES, M.A., F.S.A.,

VICE-PRESIDENT OF THE CHETHAM SOCIETY

PRINTED FOR THE CHETHAM SOCIETY.
M.DCCC.LXXV.

INTRODUCTION.

THE following Easter Rolls of the Parish of Whalley in the 6 and 7 of Edward VI., consist of ten leaves, being apparently a roll of paper with writing on both sides and now carefully preserved by being pasted in a folio manuscript volume, containing *Notes of Capitular Visitations of the exempt Jurisdiction of the Abbot and Convent of B. V. M. of Whalley*, from A.D. 1500 to 1538, which is in the library at Stonyhurst. The conventual jurisdiction embraced the royal forests of Pendle, Trawden, Rossendale, Bowland and Blackburnshire ; and the minor offences committed against good morals and the laws of the Church, as well as the subtraction of tithes and the withholding of Easter dues, were formally investigated by a jury of laymen, who assembled several times in the year, apparently as occasion served, either in the consistory within the parish church of Whalley or in the chapel of St. Michael within the castle of Clitheroe. A commissary was appointed by the abbot and convent, and he seems to have been armed with the power of summoning individuals to appear before him charged with fraudulent or immoral acts ; and proctors, who were

clerks in some of the orders of the Church, were employed
to defend the accused, if the case admitted of defence,
and sometimes, it may be inferred, when it did not.
Various other incidental cases and suits were brought
before this court, and on conviction, after evidence,
penance, restitution, and pecuniary fines were enjoined ;
but there was no rigour, nor much of the ancient dis-
cipline enforced. There is great similarity, as might
have been expected, in all these cases, and the verdicts
are in most instances the same. The commissary was
Christopher Smith, the last *prior* of the abbey, " aged upwards of four-score years" (*Lanc. MSS.*, vol. xxii, p. 489),
when he was buried in Whalley church, 5 July 1539. (*Reg.
Book.*) With his death the court and its jurisdiction pro-
bably ceased to exist, as the dissolution of the abbey was
at hand. These Rolls were prepared almost immediately
after that event by the new masters. The abbot and
convent of Whalley had been endowed *inter alia* with
the rectorial and vicarial tithes of the whole parish as
well as with the Easter dues. These latter are named
as early as the year 1395, and continued to be paid by
the parishioners until the dissolution, when they became
vested in the crown. By a deed of exchange ten years
afterwards (1547) between Edward VI. and archbishop
Cranmer the appropriate rectories of Whalley, Blackburn
and Rochdale, with their chapels, were conveyed to the
see of Canterbury, much to its disadvantage, and the
vicarage of Whalley and its filial dependencies were

abandoned to poverty; but in the year 1688 they received, as Dr. Whitaker observes, "a noble and most judicious augmentation, by a grant of the whole Easter roll and surplice fees," from archbishop Juxon, on the renewal of a lease of the tithes. At that time sir Ralph Assheton, the lessee, valued the Easter roll at 120*l.*, but it was proved to fall considerably short of that sum. The several items payable are exactly contained in an inquisition of survey taken by Roger Nowell of Read esq. and others, A.D. 1616. A small money payment seems to have been made by each parishioner at Easter as well as a commuted payment for small tithe. (*Hist. Whalley*, pp. 131, 149, 3rd ed.) It is not unworthy of remark that some of the ancient, as well as modern, parishioners of Whalley had imperfect views on the subject of sacrilege. (*Lanc. MSS.*, vol. xxii, p. 489.) We learn from these Rolls the exact number of householders in the village of Whalley and in each of its hamlets at the time of the dissolution of the abbey.

The Easter Role of Whalley in the Sext yere of the reigne of Kyng edward the sext.

Whalley.

IHON bradill	xii^{d}
Ux̄ Rychard crombock	xii^{d}
Ux̄ Rychard crauen	ii^{s} vj^{d}
James Wodd	xii^{d}
George Shuttilworth	ii^{s} vi^{d}
James chooe	ix^{d} ^{ca}
James Grenefild cū fill.	x^{d}
Robert Chatburn	v^{d}
Ux̄ Thomas chattburn cū fill.	x^{d}
Ux̄ Raffe moorton cū fill.	xiiii^{d}
Xp̄offer thorneb^{r} cū fill.	v^{d} ob̄
Lawrence hey	v^{d}
Ihon fors̄	vi^{d} ob̄
Ihon cowp	ii^{s}
Robert Lawe	iii^{s}
Henry Lawe	iiii^{d}
Xp̄offer Smyth	xx^{d}
Henry ryeley	x^{d}
Willm̄ dobson	
Robert dobson	
Edward wawen	ix^{d} ob̄
Ux̄ James myddilton cū fill.	ix^{d} ob̄
Richard carney	xiii^{d} ob̄

Ux. Edward Stanworth	... ...	j^d
Thomas mytton	... .	ii^d
Margarett wylson	... ...	ii^d
Ux. Richard crauen cū fill.	... ...	
Rog gregson	... ...	
Willm craven	... ...	v^d
Thomas forst cū fill.	... ...	v^d
Ux Rog crauen cū fill. ...	... ...	v^d
Ihon pereson	... ...	v^d
Ux Ihon browne	... .	ii^s
Thomas crauen	... ...	v^d
Edmund turñ	.. ..	iiii^d ob
Ryc hyndle	... ...	vi^d ob
thomas lickas	... ...	iiii^d
James jhonson	... ...	
Ryc hodgeson	... ...	iiii^d ob
Ryc graueson	... ...	iiii^d
James holk^r	... ...	iiii^d ob
. . . . . cartmell	... ...	iiii^d
. . illm fforst	... ...	v^d ob
. . ry bradill	... ...	vi^d
. . . . . webster	... ...	iiii^d
. . . .	... ...	v^d
	... ...	iii^d
	... ...	v^d

𝔓𝔞𝔡𝔭𝔥𝔞𝔪.

I IION Kockshote señ cū fill. ...	...	viii^d
Xpoffer bawdwen	...	viii^d
Ihon Kockshote jun.	... ...	vi^d
George fletch^r	... ...	vi^d
Adam horwich	... ...	vi^d
Rychard barrō cū fill. ...	...	ix^d
Robert whypp	...	vi^d

Willm̃ Whytehead	...	...	... viid ob
Ux̃ Willm̃ fawsett	...	...	... iiid
Franc⁸ websᵗ cu. Ryc.	...	...	... xvd
Laurence Whytakʳ Ju.	...	...	... xd
Lyonel whypp	...	...	... vid
Henry Shorrocke	...	...	... xiid
Thomas willasill	...	...	...
Ihon Denbye	...	...	... vid
Iohn Ynghᵐ	...	...	... xd ob
Ellis robinson	...	...	... iiid
Nycholas halsted	...	...	... xiiid ob
Ihon tatersall	...	...	... xd ob
Xp̃offer Deconson	...	...	... xiiid ob
Isabell cūliff	...	...	... iiiid
lavrence houghton	...	...	...
Iohn hogeson	...	...	... viiid
Xp̃offer cronkeshay	...	...	...
Ux̃ Robert ballard	...	...	...
Ux̃ henry kockshote	...	...	...
Robert kocksehote	...	...	...
James Wilkynson	...	...	...
Ric. marshall cū Ihon	...	...	... viid
Jane Sclaᵗ	...	...	...
Ryc. Wilkinson	...	...	...
. . . . . Hancoke	...	...	...
. . . . . hyndle	...	...	...

𝕾𝖙𝖆𝖓𝖉𝖊𝖓.

GILIS colthurst	...	...	... iiiis iiiid
James aspenaughe		...	... iis ixd ob
Ryc. turnor	...	...	... xiid ob
Ux. Ihon felden	...	...	... xid
Willm̃ ffarrand	...	...	... xxid

Smᵃ x⁸ xd

Hey Houses.

U X⁹ Iohn halyday	...	...	... xᵈ oƀ
geffrey filden cũ fill.		...	... xviiᵈ oƀ
Kychard Radcliff	...	...	... xiᵈ
Ryc. fort	...	...	... viiᵈ oƀ
Nycholas grymesha	...	...	... xiiiᵈ
Willm̃ halyda	. .	...	... xᵈ
Willm̃ Stones	...	...	... viiiᵈ
Edward nowell	...	...	... viiiᵈ oƀ
Rychard halyday	...	...	... xiiᵈ
Robert sterkey	...	...	... viiᵈ oƀ

Smᵃ viiiˢ ixᵈ oƀ

Loer Hygham.

N YCHOLAS hancocke	...	...	... iiˢ iiiᵈ oƀ
. . . . . bothemã	...	...	... viiiᵈ
. . . eant smyth	...	...	... viiᵈ oƀ
. . . . . banest̃	...	...	... viᵈ oƀ
. . . . r smethees	...	...	... viiiᵈ oƀ

Sm̃ᵃ iiiiˢ ixᵈ

. . . vest Clopse.

Hapton.

T HOMAS ryeley	..	...	... xxiiᵈ
Myles clayton	...	...	... xviiᵈ
Omffrey pollard	...	...	... xiiiiᵈ
Hugh Clayton	...	...	... xiiᵈ
Ihon Willson	...	...	... xiiiiᵈ oƀ
Robert whytehead	...	...	... viᵈ
Ihon Horwich	...	...	... viiiiᵈ oƀ

Edward Birtwisill ... ... xvi^d ob
Ihon Woade ... ...
Edward Robert ... ... viii^d
Willm̄ Robertshay ... ... xiii^d
U℞ George Pollard cū fil. ... ... xi^d ob
George Yate cū m̄re ... ... xvi^d ob
Willm̄ Clayton ... ... x^d
Edmund robert ... ...
James habringham ... ... ii^d
Olyu̅ bertwisill ... ... xx^d ob
Ihon Hey ... ... viii^d ob
George Wilkinson cū m̄re ... ... x^d
James bothe ... ... ix^d
James halstid ... ... xv^d
Henry Yate ... ... xii^d ob
Robert Wilkinson ... ... vi^d
Robert habryiam ... ... xvi^d
Thomas stopper ... ... vii^s ii^d
Hugh Yate ... ...
Ihon birtwisill ... ...
Henry ryeley ... ...
henry wilkinson ... ...
Ellin shirlak^r ... ...

Sm^a xxvs & . . . .

𝕾𝔂𝔪𝔬𝔫𝔰𝔱𝔬𝔫.

[6 E. VI.]

U X. Laurence Starkey ... ... xi^d
　Geffrey Hyndle ... ... ix^d
Barnard Shuttillworth ... ... vii^d ob
Edmund Yngh^{a}m ... ...
Barnard H'graue ... ... x^d
U℞ Henry Sai℣ ... ...
Edmund Kockeshote cū m̄re ... ... xiii^d

thomas whytak^r sen̄	...	...	... xi^d
U^x James Lonisdale	...	...	... xiii^d ob
Xp̄off^r Whytak^r	...	...	... x^d
Ryc. Sclat̃	...	...	.. viii^d ob
Ux. Edward robert cū fil.		...	... x^d ob
U^x Willm̃ saig̃	...	...	... ix^d
Thomas Whytak^r Ju.	...	...	... ix^d
Robert H^rgreve	...	...	... xvi^d
Edward Saig̃	...	...	... ix^d
Ihon Pollard Ju.	...	...	... i^d
Laurence Saig̃	...	...	...
Thomas Lonisdale	...	...	...
Myles Whytak^r	...	...	...
Richard . . onckshay	...	...	...
Ryc. grimsha	...	...	...
. . . .	...	...	...

Sum^a xv^s lx^d

Penulton.

[6 E. VI.]

U X. Iohn Smyth	...	...	... xiii^d
M^rgret Ots	...	...	... iiii^d
Ux. Ihon Whytehead	...	...	... ix^d
Robert Whipp	...	...	... x^d
Robert M^rsdene	...	...	... xiii^d
Thomas Hogeson	...	...	... viii^d
Ihon Hogeson	...	...	... vi^d
V^x Edmund Hogeson	...	...	... iiii^d
Ryc. tinckenele	...	...	... xv^d
Thomas Choeson	...	...	... viii^d
Willm̃ houghton	...	...	... xii^d
Willm̃ Sidgreve	...	...	... xi^d ob
Robert Caryar	...		... x^d ob
U^x Ihon grene	...		... iii^d ob

Uꝛ Willm̃ sell^r	...	...	...	x^d
Ihon bowk^r	...	...	...	xiii^d oƀ
Ihon Southworth	...	...	...	xviii^d
James Alth^am	...	...	...	vi^d oƀ
Ihon farrand	...	...	...	vii^d oƀ
Henry rossall	...	...	...	iiii^d
Rychard Wodd	...	...	...	xii^d
Willm̃ bowk^r	...	...	...	x^d
Lyonell Woulton	...	...	...	v^d
Willm̃ Whytak^r	...	...	...	vii^d oƀ
Ux. Willm̃ carryar	...	...	...	v^d oƀ
..... hogeson	...	...	...	iii^d oƀ
....	...	...	...	i^d
	...	...	..	xi^d
....	...	..	...	vi^d
..... turk	...	...	...	
.... nald wont	...	...	...	x^d
.... greves	...	...	...	xi^d oƀ
		...... ^s vii^d		

Lyttle Mytton.

GILES Hamaunt cũ m̃re	...	...	xxi^d
Uꝛ Edward colthurst	...	...	viii^d
Ihon lee	...	...	xvii^d oƀ
Ryc. dodgeson	...	...	x^d
Xp̃off^r Sell^r	...	...	ix^d oƀ
Vx. Ryc̃ whytak^r	...	...	ii^s
Robert Smythe	...	...	vii^d

Wyswall.

FRANCIS Paslaw ...		...	xiiii^d
Uꝛ Ihon Lawe ...		...	xii^d oƀ
Uꝛ Ihon Woulton	...	...	xvi^d oƀ

Robert Lawson ...	...	xv^d
U͡x Gilis grene ...	... ...	vii^d
Robert Law Ju. ...	... ...	xvii^d
Thomas Wadington ...	... ...	xvii^d oƀ
George hanson ...	... ...	xv^d
Ux. Edmund cowop ...	... ...	v^d
Ihon Hyndle ...	... ...	vii^d
Thomas Law ...	... ...	vi^d
U͡x Willm̃ Sell^r ...	... ...	iiii^d oƀ
Willm̃ grene cũ m̃re ...	... ...	
Willm̃ derwyn ...	... ...	
. . . .	... ...	
. . . .	... ...	
U͡x Ihon Dobson cũ fill.	... ...	xvi^d oƀ
Arthur wodd ...	... ...	ix^d
Rychard Pattfild ...	... ...	vi^d
Ihon wod ...	... ...	viii^d
V͡x Ryc. Dewhurst ...	... ...	xi^d oƀ
V͡x Willm̃ leghe ...	... ...	iii^d
X̃poffer Sell^r ...	... ...	viii^d
U͡x Henry Law ...	... ...	ix^d
Willm̃ law jun. ...	... ...	xiii^d oƀ
X̃poffer coke cũ patre ...	... ...	x^d
Ihon deant ...	... ...	ii^d
Willm̃ Law sen. ...	... ...	v^d oƀ
Ihon blagburne ...	... ...	vi^d oƀ
Ihon rychardson ...	... ...	iiii^d oƀ
George Huncote cũ m̃re	... ...	xii^d oƀ
Laurence high^{a}m ...	... ...	iiii^d
Robert Lany^{9}an ...	... ...	vi^d oƀ
Rychard Grene ...	... ...	v^d oƀ

Sm^a xxxi^s x^d

Reyde.

ROGER Nowell armiᵍ ... ... iiiiˢ viiiᵈ oƀ
    Ihon holkʳ ... ...
Ux. Thomas Sellʳ ... ... xiiiiᵈ oƀ
Uˣ Edward Yngᵃm ... ... xiiᵈ
Vˣ Xp̄offᵗ Dugdale ... ... viiᵈ oƀ
...... Holkʳ ... ... viiiᵈ oƀ
.... nesworth ... ... viᵈ
.... ley ... ...
....

Over bygham.

HUGH Moore ... ... xiiiᵈ
   Uˣ Ihon Moore cū fill. ... ... xvᵈ
Xp̄offʳ moore ... ... xiiiᵈ oƀ
George hargreves ... ...
Vˣ Rychard hargreves cū fil. ... ... viiᵈ oƀ
Rauffe hargreves ... ... ixᵈ
Vˣ Robert hargreves ... ... xᵈ
Edward hargreves Juñ ... ... viᵈ
Edward hargreves Señ ... ... xiiᵈ
Uˣ Lawrence hitchinson ... ...
Ihon hargreves señ ... ... xiiᵈ
Edmond Emott ... ...
James hargreves señ ... ...
Hugh hargreves .. ..
James hargreves jũ ... ... xiiᵈ
Ihon hargreves sen. ... ... viᵈ
Uˣ Robert Wytakʳ ... ...

        Smᵃ ixˢ ixᵈ

The Easter Rolle of Whalley made in the vii yere of the Reigne of Kyng Edward the sixt.

Whalley.

IOHN Braddell	xii^d
Ux Ric. crombocke	viii^d ob
Ux. Ric. craven	ii^s xi^d
James Woode	xi^d
George Shotilworth	ii^s vi^d
James Choe	viii^d
James Grenefild cũ fill.	xii^d
Robert chatborne	vii^d
Ux. Thõs chatborne	ix^d ob
Ux. Raffe murton cũ fill.	xv^d ob
Xpoffer thorneper	xii^d
Laurence hey	v^d ob
Ihon forster	v^d
Ihon cowp	ii^s
Robert lawe	iii^s
Henr Lawe	v^d ob
Xpoffer smyth	xx^d
Vx Henry ryeley	xv^d ob
Willm dobson	xvi^d ob
Robert dobson	xii^d ob
Percivall pereson	v^d
Willm Claton	xx^d
Henry holcar	x^d
Ux John holker	x^d

Willm̃ latas	...	...	...	iiii^d
UΩ thom. holden	...	...	...	vi^d ob
Robert Sagher	...	...	...	^{d} ob
Peter degne	...	...	...	^{d} ob
John gregson	...	...	...	
James lowe	...	...	...	
.... les	...	...	...	
Edward craven	...	...	...	
VΩ Iames Myddilton cũ fil.	...	...		
ryc. carny	...	...	...	iiii^d
VΩ Edward stanwarth	...	...	...	i^d
Thomas mytton	...	...	...	ii^d
Margaret wilson	...	...	...	ii^d
Willm̃ craven	...	...	...	iiii^d ob
UΩ thõas forster	...	...	...	v^d
VΩ nyc. craven	...	...	...	iii^d
John pereson	...	...	...	iii^d
VΩ Iohn broune	...	...	...	ii^d ob
Thomas craven	...	...	...	v^d ob
Edmund turñ	...	...	...	viii^d
Ric. hindle	...	...	...	vi^d
Thomas Lycas	...	...	...	iiii^d
James Johnson	...	...	...	vi^d
Ric. hodgeson	...	...	...	iiii^d ob
Ric. graveson	...	...	...	iiii^d ob
James holk^r	...	...	...	iii^d ob
John Cartmell &	...	...	...	
Willm̃ forster	...	...	...	vi^d
Henr̃ Bradell	...	...	...	vi^d
Robert Wolfenden	...	...	...	iiii^d ob
Willm̃ m'cer	...	...	...	viii^d ob
Seth Pereson	...	...	...	iii^d ob
Willm̃ cowpe	...	...	...	v^d ob
Thomas lawe juñ	...	...	...	i^d ob

Ric. forsᵗ   ...   .   iiiiᵈ
Iohn Brown cū m̄re   ...   .   viᵈ
Robert Sharplus   ...   .

Smᵃ Lˢ

Padiħᵃm.

[Aᵒ vii r. E. VI.]

xᵈ	VXᵍ Henry Wytaker ...	...	
xviᵈ	Laurens Whitaker señ	...	
ixᵈ oƀ	Hugh Shotilworth	...	...
viiiᵈ	John Hey	...	...
	Edmund nutᵗ	...	...
iiᵈ oƀ	Vᵕ Wilm̄ Hodgeson	...	...
viiᵈ oƀ	Xp̄o. Robinson cū m̄re	...	... xiiiᵈ
viᵈ	John Wilkinson	...	... viiᵈ
ixᵈ	Robert Houghton cū m̄re	...	... xᵈ
xᵈ oƀ	Henri Birtwisill	...	... xᵈ
viᵈ	Henry Dodgeson	...	... ixᵈ
viᵈ	Ric. Ballard	...	... vᵈ
	Lawrens cockeshott	...	... viᵈ
	Vᵕ Nycholas forster	...	...
xiᵈ	Xp̄offer Dodgeson cū m̄re	...	... xviᵈ
iiiiᵈ	Vᵕ Willm̄ Wallshame	...	... viᵈ
	John Aspeden	...	...
vᵈ	Giles Slaᵗ	...	... iiiᵈ
ixᵈ	Willm̄ nowell	...	... viiiᵈ
xᵈ	Vᵕ Thöas mʳshall	...	... xᵈ oƀ
	Robert Dodgeson	...	... viᵈ
viiᵈ	Thöas whippe	...	... viiiᵈ
viᵈ	Ric. Shenfild	...	...
xiᵈ	Jamys Willk	...	...
ixᵈ	John	...	...

...

...

Ɗapton.

vi^s	Edward Asheton (demysed)	...	v^x
x^d	Thomas Reley	...	...
xiii^d	Miles Clayton	...	...
xi^d	Omfrey pollard	...	...
xii^d oƀ	Hugh clayton	...	...
xv^d	John Willson	...	...
viii^d oƀ	Robert Whitched	...	...
ix^d	George horwiche cū m̄re	...	
xx^d	Edmond birtwisell	...	...
	John woode	...	...
ix^d oƀ	Edward Roberts	...	...
xii^d	Willm̄ Robertshawe	...	...
xviii^d oƀ	Ux̄ George pollard cū fil.	...	
xvi^d oƀ	George Yate cū m̄re	...	...
x^d	Willm̄ clayton	...	...
x^d	Edmonde Robert	...	...
ii^d	James Habrinjame	...	...
xviii^d oƀ	Olyv̄ Birtwisill	...	...
xi^d	John Hey	...	...
vi^d	Thomas Wilkynson cū m̄re	...	
xii^d	James Bothe	...	. .
xix^d oƀ	James Halstid	...	...
	Henry Yate	...	... xii^d
	.. bert Wilkynson	...	... vi^d
	.... injame	...	...

Lyttill Mytton.

G ILES Hammond cũ m̃re ... ...
.... Edward Colthurst ... ...
.... lce ... ...
.... dodgeson ... ...
Thomas sonkey ... ... x^d
....
....

Penulton.

[7 E. VI.]

U X^9 John Smyth	...	...	...
Margaret Otes	...	..	...
U𝔵 Iohn Whitehed	...	...	...
Robert Whippe	...	...	...
Robert Marsden	...	...	...
Thomas Hodgeson	...	...	x^d
Iohn Hodgeson	...	...	...
U𝔵 Edmund Hodgeson		...	...
Ric̨ tyncknell	...	...	x^d
Willm̃ Avensen	...	...	x^d
Willm̃ houghton	...	...	x^d
Robert cariar	...	...	x^d
U𝔵 Iohn Grene	...	...	iii^d
U𝔵 Willm̃ Sell^r	...	...	vi^d
Iohn Bowk^r	...	...	vii^d
Iohn Sothworth	...	...	x^d
Iames Alltha m	...	...	xii^d
Iohn farrand	...	...	xii^d
Henry Rossall	...	...	iiii^d
Ric̨ Wode	...	...	xii^d
Willm̃ Bowker	...	...	viii^d
Lyonell Woulton	...	...	v^d

Willm̃ Whytak^r ... ...

Ux̃ Willm̃ coore ... ...

James Hodgeson ... ...

Oliver Whippe ... ...

𝔖𝔶𝔪𝔬𝔫𝔰𝔱𝔬𝔫.

[7 E. VI.]

U X⁹ Laurence Starky ... ... viii^d

Geffrey Hyndle ... ... x^d

Barnard Shothilworth ... ... viii^d oƀ

Edmund Yygham ... ...

Barnard H⁹greves ... ... xiii^d

Edmund Cockeshot cũ m̃re ... ... xiii^d

Thomas Whytaker sen̄ ... ... xv^d

Ux̃ Iames Londisdale ... ... xi^d

Ux̃ Xp̃offer Whitak^r ... ... xiii^d

Ux̃ Ric. Slaȓ .. .. viii^d

Ux. Edward Robert cũ fill. ... ... x^d oƀ

Ux̃ Willm̃ Saigher ... ... x^d

Thomas Whitaker Jun̄ ... ... xi^d oƀ

Ux̃ Robert Hergreves ... ... xvii^d

Edward Saigher ... ... ix^d

Iohn Pollard Jun̄ ... ... vii^d

Laurence Saigher ... ... i^d

Iohn Hgreves cũ Laurence ... ... x^d

Thomas Lonsdale ... ... x^d

Myles Whitaker ... ... xiii^d

Ryc. Gudshawe ... ... v^d

Ux̃ Henry Saigher ... ...

Sum̃^a xvii^s v^d

Reade.

R OGER Nowell armiǧ ... ...
   Iohn Holk^r ... ...
U̱ Thõas Sell^r ... ... xvii^d
Edward Yngh^am ... ...
U̱ X̃poffcr Dugedale ... ... vii^d
Rondle Holcar ... ... x^d oḃ
Iohn Aynysworth ... ... xii^d
Ric. Hornebye ... ... ix^d
Henry Ryeley ... ... ix^d
Ric. Hodgeson ... ... ix^d
Robert Yngh^am ... ... xi^d
U̱ X̃poffcr Norram ... ... xii^d
Nyc̃ P'ker ... ... ix^d
X̃poffcr haliday ... ...
Thomas Yngh^am ... ... xvii^d
Iohn Browne ... ... xi^d
Iohn Norram ... . xi^d
James Holt cũ fill. ... ... viii^d
Thomas Sonkey ... . xi^d
Iohn m^rc̃ ... ... vi^d
Iohn tomasson ... ...
Iohn Oldfelde cũ m̃re ... ... x^d
Willm̃ gooden ... ...
George romsbottom ... ...
Margery Nowell ... ...
Anes simson ... ...
Robart holden ... ... i^d oḃ

Sum^a xxii^s viii^d

Wiswall.

[7 E. VI.]

FRANCIS Paslowe	...	...	xv^d
Uх Iohn Lawe	...	...	ix^d
Uх Iohn Woulton	...	...	xx^d
Robert Lawe sen	...	...	xvi^d
Robert Lawe jun	...	...	xvi^d
Thomas Wadington	...	...	xvii^d
George Hawston	...	...	xxiii^d
Uх Edmund Cowpe	...	...	v^d ob
Iohn Hindle	...	...	vii^d ob
Thomas Lane	..	...	
Uх Willm Seller	...	...	vi^d
William Grene cū m̄re	...	. .	xi^d
Willm Derwyn	...	..	xiii^d
Iohn Lawe	...	...	ii^d
Uх Willm Radcliffe	...	...	vii^d
Robert Smyth	...	...	x^d
Thomas Dobson .	...	...	
Ric. Dobson	...	...	v^d ob
Ric. thropp	...	...	viii^d
Robert giles	...	...	vii^d ob
Omfrey Dodgeson	...	...	xiii^d
George Grene	...	...	v^d ob
Iohn Radcliffe	...	...	v^d ob
Robert Craven	...	...	ix^d
Thōas belinge	...	...	
Ux. John Dobson cū fil.	...	...	xiii^d
Arthure Wode	...	...	viii^d
Ric. hatfilde	...	...	viii^d
Iohn Wode	...	...	xi^d
Uх Ric. Dewhurst	...	...	xiii^d
Uх Willm Lee	...		

D

X̄poffer Seller ... ...

U͞x Edmund Lawe ... ...

Willm̄ Lawe jun. ... ...

X̄poffer Coke cū p̄re ... ...

John Doson ... ...

Willm̄ Lawe sen. ... ...

John Blackborne ... ...

John Ric̓son ... ...

George Huncote cū m̄re ... ...

Laurence In.... ... ...

Robert ....

U͞x Iohn Ellot . . ..

Laurence hanson ... ... v^{d}

Nycholas Shore ... ... vii^{d}

Thomas Whyttak^{r} ... ... vii^{d} oƀ

George conkeshay ... ... ix^{d}

Willm̄ Walshay ... ... iiii^{d}

Yeom p'ker ... ...

Margaret cronckshay ... ...

The Thirty-Second Report

OF THE

COUNCIL OF THE CHETHAM SOCIETY,

Read at the Annual Meeting, held, by permission of the Feoffees,
in the Audit Room of Chetham's Hospital, on Wednesday,
the 3rd day of March, 1875, by adjournment
from the 1st of March.

THE first and second of the publications for the year 1874–5, and the 93rd and 94th in the Chetham Series, consist of Parts 1 and 2 of the third and concluding volume of *The Admission Register of the Manchester School*, with some Notices of the more distinguished Scholars, by the Rev. JEREMIAH FINCH SMITH, M.A., Rector of Aldridge, Staffordshire.

This concluding volume carries on the *Register* from the death of Mr. Lawson in 1807 to the resignation of the High Mastership by Dr. Jeremiah Smith, in Michaelmas 1837. An appendix of Addenda, containing new notices of Scholars and additions to those previously given, extending from page 288 to 343, and a list of Portraits presented to the School by the Editor, is subjoined.

The Council cannot but congratulate the Members on the completion of this very valuable work, the result of untiring labour and perseverance. No other School in the Kingdom can boast of a biographical record of its Scholars approaching in the slightest degree, in point of copiousness and accuracy of detail, to that which Mr. Smith has supplied for the period which it embraces with respect to Bishop Oldham's foundation. He has enriched not merely local, but general, biography by very large accessions of the most interesting kind, and for which all those who duly appreciate the value and importance of that delightful branch of Historical Literature are bound to be proportionately grateful. The last volume will be acknowledged by its readers to yield in no respect as regards its variety of attraction and fulness of information to either of those which preceded it.

The concluding prefatory remark of the Editor, that he is not without hope that he may be able at some future day to put forth, under the auspices of the CHETHAM SOCIETY, some similar notices of distinguished men educated at the School previously to 1730, as well as of the Masters of the School from its foundation, will be received with general satisfaction by all the members of the CHETHAM SOCIETY. For the five illustrative plates contained in this volume — the portraits of Bishop Oldham, Mr. Lawson and Dr. Smith, and the views of Bishop Oldham's tomb, and the Residential house — the members are indebted to the liberality of the Editor.

The third work for the year 1874-5, forming No. 95 in the Chetham Series, is *Christopher Towneley's Abstracts of Lancashire Inquisitions.* Edited by WILLIAM LANGTON, Esq. Part 1. The Council feel satisfied that the appearance of this long-looked-for publication from the MS. volumes of the indefatigable transcriber and antiquary, Christopher Towneley, will be hailed with no common pleasure by those who feel interested in the family and territorial History of Lancashire. The information derived from these inquisitions, which extend in the present part from the 25th of Edward I. to the 3rd of Henry IV., it is almost needless to observe is of the most genuine and authentic kind, and the slightest glance at the contents is sufficient to show what valuable materials they supply to the local Historian and Genealogist and what effectual aid they must afford to Lancashire Antiquarian investigation. They have the great advantage of having in Mr. Langton an Editor who is thoroughly and profoundly conversant with the subject, and whose full and accurate illustrative remarks and pedigrees add very considerably to the usefulness of the publication.

The publications contemplated, or in progress, are :

1. *Christopher Towneley's Lancashire Inquisitions.* Edited by WILLIAM LANGTON, Esq. Part 2.

2. *Chetham Miscellanies.* Vol. 5.

3. *Collectanea Anglo-Poetica,* Part 6. By the Rev. THOMAS CORSER, M.A., F.S.A.

4. *Worthington's Diary and Correspondence.* The concluding part. Edited by JAMES CROSSLEY, Esq., F.S.A., President of the Chetham Society.

5. *Contributions to the History of the Parish of Prestbury, co. Chester.* By FRANK RENAUD, M.D.

6. *The Lancashire Visitation of* 1532. Edited by WILLIAM LANGTON, Esq.

7. *History of the Ancient Chapel of Stretford, in Manchester Parish, together with Notices of the more ancient local Families.* Edited by JAMES CROSTON, Esq.

8 *Biographical Collectanea regarding Humphrey Chetham and his family.* By the Rev. CANON RAINES, M.A., F.S.A.

9. *Documents relating to Edward third Earl of Derby and the Pilgrimage of Grace.* By R. C. CHRISTIE, Esq., M.A.

10. *A Selection from the Letters of Dr. Dee, with an introduction of Collectanea relating to his Life and Works.* By THOMAS JONES, B.A., F.S.A., Librarian of Chetham's Library.

11. *Correspondence of Nathan Walworth and Peter Seddon of Outwood, and other Documents and Papers in relation to the building of Ringley Chapel.* Prepared for the press by the late ROBERT SCARR SOWLER, Esq. Q.C.

12. *Poem upon the Earls and Barons of Chester,* in 62 octave stanzas from an ancient MS. belonging to John Arden, Esq., of Stockport, believed to have been written by Richard Bostock of Tattenhall, gent.; a copy of which is in a MS. volume written by the Rev. John Watson, rector of Stockport, M.A., F.S.A., and from this the present transcript was taken.

13. A republication, with an introductory notice, of *A true Narrative of the Proceedings in the several Suits in Law that have been between the Right Honble Charles Lord Gerard of Brandon, and A. Fitton, Esq.,* by a Lover of Truth, 4to, printed at the Hague, 1663; and the other tracts relating to the same subject.

14. *Selections from the Correspondence of Sir William Brereton relating to affairs in the county of Chester during the Civil Wars.* From the originals contained in seven large folio volumes in the British Museum.

15. *A Collection of Ancient Ballads and Poems, relating to Lancashire.*

16. *Diary of John Angier, of Denton, from the original Manuscripts, with a reprint of the Narrative of his Life published in 1685 by Oliver Heywood.*

17. *A Selection from Dr. John Byrom's unprinted Remains in Prose and Verse.*

18. *A new Edition of the Poems Collected and Published after his Death, corrected and revised, with Notes, and a Prefatory Sketch of his Life.*

19. *Hollinworth's Mancuniensis.* A new edition. Edited by CANON RAINES.

20. *A Volume of Extracts, Depositions, Letters, &c., from the Consistory Court of Chester, beginning with the Foundation of the See.*

21. *Extracts from Roger Dodsworth's Collections in the Bodleian Library at Oxford relating to Lancashire.*

22. *Annales Cestrienses.*

23. *A General Index to volumes XXXI. to C. of the Publications of the Chetham Society.*

THE TREASURER IN ACCOUNT WITH THE CHETHAM SOCIETY,

Dr.　　　　*For the Year ending February 28th, 1874.*　　　　**Cr.**

	£	s.	d.
1 Subscription for 1868-69 (26th year), reported in arrear at last meeting.			
3 Subscriptions for 1869-70 (27th year), reported in arrear at last meeting.			
5 Subscriptions for 1870-71 (28th year), reported in arrear at last meeting.			
2 Collected	2	0	0
3 Outstanding.			
9 Subscriptions for 1871-72 (29th year), reported in arrear at last meeting.			
4 Collected	4	0	0
5 Outstanding.			
28 Subscriptions for 1872-73 (30th year), reported in arrear at last meeting.			
14 Collected	14	0	0
14 Outstanding.			
80 Subscriptions for 1873-74 (31st year), reported in arrear at last meeting.			
1 less, included in books sold.			
79			
51 Collected	51	0	0
28 Outstanding.			
73 Subscriptions for 1874-5 (32nd year), reported at the last meeting.			
179 Collected	179	0	0
41 Compounders			
57 Arrears.			
350			
30 { 2 Subscriptions for 1875-76 (33rd year), reported at last meeting.			
28 Do. do. paid in advance...........	28	0	0
1 Subscription for 1876-77 (34th year), reported at last meeting.			
1 Subscription for 1877-78 (35th year), reported at last meeting.			
1 Subscription for 1878-79 (36th year), reported at last meeting.			
1 Subscription for 1879-80 (37th year), reported at last meeting.*			
1 Subscription for 1880-81 (38th year), reported at last meeting.*			
1 Subscription for 1881-82 (39th year), paid in advance.	1	0	0
1 Subscription for 1882-83 (40th year), paid in advance.	1	0	0
Books sold to Members (including £45 19 8 received by C. Simms & Co.)	126	15	4
Consol Dividends	7	8	10
Bank Interest	7	7	0
	£421	11	2
Balance brought forward March 1st 1874.	252	4	3
	£673	15	5

		£	s.	d.
1874.				
June 27	County Office, Fire Insurance	3	15	0
Oct. 17	Books bought, per Mr. Crossley....	8	1	0
Dec. 29	C. Simms & Co.:			
	Vol. 92. ....£140 4 0			
	Vol. 93. .... 136 15 6			
	Vol. 94. .... 146 18 9			
	General Printing and Postages 11 15 0			
		435	13	3
1875.				
Jan. 30	Copies of letters &c. in the Bodleian.	2	1	0
Feb. 5	Mr. Quaritch, commission on books delivered to members	10	16	0
Feby. 28	Balance in the Bank.................	£460	6	3
		213	9	2
		£673	15	5

* In the last statement 2 subscriptions quoted in error.

March 12th, 1875.　Audited and found correct.

GEORGE PEEL.
GEORGE THORLEY.
HENRY M. ORMEROD.

ARTHUR H. HEYWOOD, *Treasurer.*

Chetham Society.

LIST OF MEMBERS

For the Year 1875—1876.

The Members, to whose names an asterisk is prefixed, have compounded for their Subscriptions.

---

* ACKERS, B. St. John, Prinknash Park, Painswick
Ainsworth, Ralph F., M.D., F.L.S., Manchester
Allen, Joseph, Tombland, Norwich
*Amhurst, W. A. Tyssen, F.S.A., Didlington Park, Brandon
*Armitage, Samuel, Pendleton, Manchester
Armstrong, Rev. Alfred Thomas, M.A., Ashton Parsonage, Preston
Armytage, Geo. J., F.S.A., Clifton, Brighouse
Ashton, John, Warrington
Ashworth, Henry, The Oaks, near Bolton
Ashworth, John W., Pendleton
Assheton, Ralph, M P., Downham Hall, Clitheroe
Atherton, James, Swinton House, near Manchester
Atkin, William, Little Hulton, near Bolton
Atkinson, William, Claremont, Southport
Avison, Thomas, F.S.A., Liverpool

B AGSHAW, John, Manchester
Bailey, John E., Stretford.
Bain, James, 1, Haymarket, London
Baker, Thomas, Skerton House, Old Trafford
*Barbour, Robert, Bolesworth Castle, near Chester
Barker, John, Broughton Lodge, Newton in Cartmel
*Barlow, Mrs., Greenhill, Oldham
Barton, Richard, Caldy Manor, Birkenhead
Beamont, William, Orford Hall, Warrington
Beever, James F., Bryn Celyn, Beaumaris
Bennett, Captain H. A., Nelson House, Manchester
Beswicke, Mrs., Pyke House, Littleborough
Birkett, Alfred, Wigan
Birley, Hugh, M.P., Moorlands, near Manchester
Birley, Rev. J. Shepherd, M.A., Halliwell Hall, Bolton
*Birley, Thomas H., Hart Hill, Eccles, Manchester
Bolderson, John, Strangeways, Manchester
Blackburne, Coln. Ireland, Hale, near Warrington

Booker, Rev. John, M.A., F.S.A., Sutton, Surrey
Booth, John, Greenbank, Monton, Eccles
Booth, William, Holly Bank, Cornbrook, Manchester
Bower, Miss, Old Park, Bostol, Abbey Wood, London S.E
Bradley, W. H., Alderley Edge
Braybrooke, Stephen H. Crumpsall
*Bridgeman, Hon. and Rev. George T. O., M A., Hon. Canon of Manchester, Wigan
Bridson, J. Ridgway, Bridge House, Bolton
Brierley, Rev. J., M A., Mosley Moss Hall, Congleton
*Brooke, Thomas, Armitage Bridge, near Huddersfield
*Brooks, W. Cunliffe, M.P., M.A., F.S.A., Barlow Hall Manchester
Brown, Mrs., Winckley Square, Preston
Browne, William Henry, St. Martin's, Chester
Buckley, Sir Edmund, Bart., M.P., Dinas Mowddwy

* CHADWICK, Elias, M.A., Pudlestone Court, Leominster
Chichester, The Lord Bishop of
Chorlton, Thomas, Brazennose Street, Manchester
Christie, The Worshipful Richard Copley, M.A., Chancellor of the Diocese of Manchester.
*Churchill, W. S., Brinnington Lodge, near Stockport
*Clare, John Leigh, Liverpool
Clarke, Archibald William, Scotscroft, Didsbury
Clegg, Thomas, Southport
Cockayne, G. E., M A., F.S.A, Lancaster Herald College of Arms, London
Colley, T. Davies-, M.D, Chester
Cooke, Thomas, Rusholme Hall, near Manchester
Corser, Rev. Thomas, M.A., F.S.A., Stand, near Manchester
*Cottam, Samuel, F.R.A.S., Wightwick House, Manchester

Coulthart, John Ross, Ashton-under-Lyne
Cowie, The Very Rev. B. M., B.D., F.S.A., Dean of Manchester
*Crawford and Balcarres, The Earl of, Haigh Hall, near Wigan
Crompton, Samuel, M.D., Manchester
Cross, Col. W. Assheton, Red Scar, Preston
Crosse, Thomas Bright, Shaw Hill, near Chorley
Crossley, George F., Beech Tree Bank. Prestwich
Crossley, James, F.S.A., Manchester, *President*
Croston, James, F.S A., Upton Hall, Prestbury
Cunningham, William Alexander, Manchester

DARBISHIRE, G. Stanley, Riversfield, Eccles
Darbishire, Mrs. S. D., Pendyffryn, near Conway
Davies, D. Reynolds, Agden Hall, Lymm
Delamere, The Lord, Vale Royal, near Northwich
*Derby, The Earl of, Knowsley, Prescot
Devonshire, The Duke of, Holker Hall, Grange, Lancashire
Dillon, Lin, Manchester
Dixon, Jas., Ormskirk
Dobson, William, Preston
Doxey, Rev. J. S, Burnley
Drake, Sir William, F S.A., Oatlands Lodge, Weybridge
Duckett, Sir George, Bart., F.S.A., Weald Manor House, Bampton, Oxford

EARLE, Frederic William, Edenhurst, near Huyton
Earwaker, J. P., F.S.A., Manchester
Eastwood, J. A., Manchester
Eccles, Richard, Wigan
Eckersley, N., Standish Hall, Wigan
Egerton, Sir Philip de Malpas Grey-, Bart., M.P., Oulton Park, Tarporley
Egerton, The Lord, Tatton Park, Knutsford
Ellesmere, The Earl of, Worsley Hall
Ellison, Cuthbert E., Worship Street, London

*FENTON, James, M.A., F.S.A., Norton Hall, Mickleton Chipping Campden, Gloucestershire
ffarington, Miss, Worden Hall, near Preston
Fielden, Joshua, M.P., Nutfield Priory, Redhill, Surrey
*Fielden, Samuel, Centre Vale, Todmorden
Fisher, William, Lancaster Banking Co., Preston
Fishwick, Lieut-Colonel, F.S.A., Carr Hill, Rochdale
Fleming, William, M.D., Rowton Grange, Chester
Forster, John, Palace Gate House, Kensington, London
Foster Joseph, Boundary Road, London

GARNETT, Wm. James, Quernmore Park, Lancaster
Gladstone, Murray, F.R.A.S, Manchester
Greaves, Hilton, Derker, Oldham
*Greenall, Gilbert, M.P., Walton Hall, near Warrington
Grover, J. N. K., Ivy Cottage, Swinton

HADFIELD, George, M.P., Manchester
Hailstone, Edward, F.S.A., Walton Hall, Wakefield
Hargreaves, George J., Piccadilly, Manchester

Harris, George, F.S.A., Isclipps Manor, Northott, Southall
Harrison, William, Rock Mount, St. John's, Isle of Man
*Harrison, William, F.S.A., F G.S, F.R.S., Antq. du Nord. Samlesbury Hall, near Preston
Harter, James Collier, Leamington
Hatton, James, Richmond House, near Manchester
Haworth, William, Burnley
Healey, Henry, Smallbridge, Rochdale
Heginbotham, Henry, Millgate House, Stockport
*Henry, W. C., M.D., F R.S., Haflield, near Ledbury
Herford, Rev. Brooke, Manchester
Heron, Rev. George, M.A., Carrington, Cheshire
Heywood, Arthur Henry, Manchester, *Treasurer*
Heywood, Rev. Henry R., M.A, Swinton, Manchester
Heywood, James, F.R.S., F.G.S., 26, Palace Gardens, Kensington, London
Heywood, Sir Thos. Percival, Bart., Doveleys, Ashbourne
Hickson, Thomas, Melton Mowbray
Higson, James, Ardwick Green North, Manchester
Higson, John, Birch Cottage, Lees, near Oldham
Hilton, William Hughes, Booth Street, Manchester
Hoare, P. R., Luscombe, Dawlish
*Hoghton, Sir Henry de, Bart., Hoghton Tower
Holden, Thomas, Springfield, Bolton-le-Moors
Holdsworth, Charles J, Eccles
Hornby, Rev. Canon, B.D., Rectory, Bury
Hornby, Rev. William, M.A., St. Michael's, Garstang, Hon. Canon of Manchester
Howard, Edward C., Brinnington Hall, Stockport
Howarth, Henry H., F S.A., Derby House, Eccles
*Hughes, Thomas, F.S.A., Grove Terrace, Chester
*Hulton, Rev. C. G., M.A., Emberton, Newport Pagnel
Hulton, W. A., Hurst Grange, Preston
Hume, Rev. A., LL.D., D.C.L., F.S.A., Liverpool
Hutchinson, Robert Hopwood, Tenter House, Rochdale

JACSON, Charles R., Barton Hall, Preston
Johnson, Jabez, Kenyon Hall, near Manchester
Johnson, W. R., The Cliffe, Wybunbury, Nantwich
Jones, Jos., Abberley Hall, Stourport
Jones, Thomas, B.A., F.S.A., Chetham Library, Manchester
Jones, Wm. Roscoe, Athenæum, Liverpool
Jordan, Joseph J., Scedley Mount, Pendleton

KAY, Samuel, Oakley House, Weaste, Manchester
Kelly, David, Stretford, near Manchester
Kemp, George T., Rochdale
Kennedy, Jno. Lawson, Ardwick Hall, Manchester
Kershaw, James, Manchester
Kershaw, John, Cross Gate, Audenshaw

LANGTON, William, Manchester
Law, Wm., Bent House, Littleborough
Lees, T. Evans, Hathershaw, Oldham
Lees, William, St. Ann's Street, Manchester
Legh, G. Cornwall, F.G.S., High Legh, Knutsford

*Leigh, Colonel Egerton, M.P., West Hall, High Leigh
Leigh, Henry, Moorfield, Swinton
Leigh, Miss, The Limes, Birkdale, Southport
Library, Bacup Co-operative Stores
—— Berlin Royal
—— Birmingham Central Free
—— Blackburn Free Public
—— Bolton Public
—— Boston, U.S., Athenæum
—— Boston, U.S., Public
—— British Museum
—— Bury Co-operative Society
—— Cambridge, Christ's College
—— Cambridge University
—— Dublin University
—— Edinburgh Advocates'
—— Gottingen University
—— Leeds
—— Liverpool Athenæum
—— Liverpool Free Public
—— Liverpool, St. Edward's College
—— London Athenæum Club
—— London Honbl. Society, Middle Temple
—— London, St. James's Square
—— London Reform Club
—— London Society of Antiquaries
—— London Zion College
—— Manchester Chetham
—— Manchester Free
—— Manchester Independent College
—— Manchester Owens College
—— Manchester Portico
—— Manchester Royal Exchange
—— Manchester Union Club
—— Oxford, Brasenose College
—— Oxford University
—— Preston, Shepherd's
—— Rochdale
—— Rochdale Co-operative Stores
—— Rochdale Free
—— Southport Free
—— Watkinson, Hartford, U.S.
—— Washington U.S. Congress
—— Windsor Royal
—— York Subscription, York
Lingard, John R., Manchester
Lingard, R. B. M., Cheetham Hill, Manchester
Litler, H. W., Wallerscote, Leamington
Lowe, James, Chorlton-cum-Hardy
Lowndes, Edward C., Castle Combe, Chippenham
*Loyd, Edward, Lillesden, Hawkhurst, Kent
*Loyd, Lewis, Monks Orchard, West Wickham, Kent
Lycett, W. E., Manchester

McCLURE, William Lees, Kersal Clough, Higher Broughton
MacKenzie, John W., Royal Circus, Edinburgh
*Manchester, The Lord Bishop of
Mann, William, Manchester
Mare, E. R. Le, Manchester
*Marriott, John, Liverpool

Marsden, G. E., Manchester
Marsden, Rev. Canon, B.D., F.R.G.S., Gt. Oakley-Harwich
*Marsh, John Fitchett, Hardwick House, Chepstow
Marshall, George W., F.S.A., Hanley Court, Tenbury
Mason, Hugh, Groby Lodge, Ashton-under-Lyne
Massie, Rev. E., M.A., Grange-over-Sands, Fleetwood
Masters, Rev. George S., West Dean Rectory, Salisbury
Mayer, Joseph, F.S.A., Lord-street, Liverpool
Metcalfe, Walter C., Epping, Essex
Milne, H. Travis, Crompton Hall, Rochdale
Milne, J. L., Lancaster
Mosley, Sir Tonman, Bart., Rolleston Hall, Staffordshire
*Moss, Rev. John James, Otterspool, Liverpool
Moult, William, Parkside, Prescot
Murray, James, Manchester

NAYLOR, Miss, Altrincham
—— *Neild, Colonel Jonathan, Rochdale
Newall, Henry, Hare Hill, Littleborough.
Newall, H. G. F., Hare Hill, Littleborough
*Newbery, Henry, Docklands, Ingatestone, Essex
Nicholson, James, F.S.A., Thelwall Hall, Warrington

ORMEROD, Rev. T. Johnson, Sedbury Park, Chepstow
Ormerod, Henry Mere, Manchester
Owen, John, Stretford Road, Manchester

*PARKER, Robert Townley, Cuerden Hall, near Preston
Parkinson, Major General, West Well House, Streatham Common, Surrey
Pedder, Richard, Preston
Peel, George, Brookfield, Cheadle
Peel, Jonathan, Knowlemere Manor, near Clitheroe
Pemberton, Richard L., The Barnes, Sunderland
Perkes, Rowland J., M.A., St. John's College, Cambridge
Perris, John, Lyceum, Liverpool
Philippi, Frederick Theod., Belfield Hall, near Rochdale
*Philips, Mark, The Park, Manchester
Picton, J. A., F.S.A., Clayton Square, Liverpool
Pierpoint, Benjamin, St. Austin's, Warrington
Pitcairn, Rev. J. P., M.A., Vicarage, Eccles
Prescott, J. B., Manchester
Price, Rev. Henry H., M.A., Ash Parsonage, Whitchurch

QUARITCH, Bernard, Piccadilly, London

RADFORD, Richard, Manchester
—— Radford, Thomas, M.D., Higher Broughton
Raine, Rev. James, M.A., Canon of York
Raines, Rev. F. R., M.A., F.S.A., Vicar of Milnrow and Hon. Canon of Manchester, *Vice President*
Raines, Rev. R. E. H., B.A., Worcester College, Oxford
Ramsbotham, James, Crowboro' Warren, Tunbridge Wells
Redhead, R. Milne, F.L.S., F.R.G.S., Seedley, Manchester

Reiss, Mrs., Broom House, near Manchester
Renaud, Frank, M.D., Piccadilly, Manchester
Reynolds, Rev. George W., M A., Cheetham Hill
Rhodocanakis, H. H. The Prince, C.K.G, Ph D.,
    F.S.A.A, F.G.H.S.
Rickards, Charles H., Manchester
Rigby, Samuel, Bruch Hall, Warrington
Roberts, Alfred Wm., Aylestone Hill, Hereford
*Roberts, Chas. H. Crompton, Upper Avenue Road,
    Regent's Park, London
Robinson, Dixon, Clitheroe Castle, Clitheroe
Roper, William, Lancaster
Rostron, Simpson, Beddington Lane, Mitcham
Royds, Albert Hudson, Malvern
Royle, Alan, Hartford Hill, near Northwich
Rushton, James, Forest House, Newchurch
Rylands, J. Paul, F.S.A., Highfields, Thelwall
Rylands, W. H., Highfields, Thelwall
Rymer Thomas, Cheetham Hill

SALISBURY, Enoch Gibbon, Glan Aber, Chester
    Sandbach, John E., Withington
*Scholes, Thomas Seddon, Dale Street, Leamington
Sharp, John, The Hermitage, Lancaster*
Shaw, George, St. Chad's, Upper Mills, Saddleworth
Shaw, James B., Apsley Terrace, Cornbrook
Shuttleworth, Sir J. P. Kay-, Bart., M.D., Gawthorpe
    Hall, Burnley
Simms, Charles E., Manchester
Simpson, John Hope, Bank of Liverpool, Liverpool
Simpson, Rev. Samuel, M.A., Newlands, Frenchay,
    Bristol
Skaife, John, Union Street, Blackburn
Skelmersdale, The Lord, Lathom House, near Ormskirk
Smith, Fereday, Manchester
Smith, J. Gibb, Oxford Road, Manchester
Smith, J. R., Soho Square, London
Smith, Rev. J. Finch, M.A., Aldridge Rectory, near
    Walsall
Smith, R. M., Mount House, Broughton
Sotheran, H., Strand, London
Sotheran, H. and Co., Strand, London
Sowler, Mrs., Sawrey Knotts, Windermere
Sowler, Thomas, Manchester
Spafford, George, Brown Street, Manchester
Standish, W. S. C., Duxbury Hall, Chorley
*Stanley of Alderley, The Lord, Alderley
Starkie, Major Le Gendre, Huntroyd
Sudlow, John, Manchester
Swindells, G. H., Heaton Chapel, Stockport

TABLEY, The Lord de, Tabley House, Knutsford
    Tatton, Thos. W., Wythenshawe Hall, Cheshire

Taylor, James, Whiteley Hall, Wigan
*Taylor, Mrs. Emily, Clive, Bournemouth
Taylor, Rev. W. H., M.A., Farnworth
Taylor, Thomas Frederick, Böderw, St.Asaph, N.Wales
Taylor, Henry. Barton House, Patricroft
Thicknesse, Rev. F. H., M.A., Hon. Canon of Man-
    chester, Beech Hill, Wigan
Thomas, Rev. D It, M A., Cefn Rectory, St. Asaph
Thompson, James, Chronicle Office, Leicester
*Thompson, Joseph, Woodlands, Fulshaw
Thorley, George, Manchester
Thorp, Henry, Whalley Range, Manchester
Tonge, Rev. Richard, M.A., Aucklands, Fallowfield
Towneley, Colonel Chas, F S.A.,Towneley Park, Burnley
Townend, John, Shadsworth Hall, Blackburn
Trafford, Sir Humphrey de, Bart., Trafford Park, Man-
    chester
Turner, John Woodville, Lytham

VAUGHAN, John Lingard, Stockport
    Vitré, Edward Denis de, M.D., Lancaster

WALKER, Rev. J. Russell, M.A., Ringley
    Walmsley, Charles, Barsham House, Malvern
Wanklyn, William Trevor, Manchester
Warburton, R. E. Egerton-, Arley Hall, near Northwich
*Ward, Jos. Pilkington, Whalley Range, Manchester
Ware, Titus Hibbert, Southport
Westhead, Joshua P. Brown, Lea Castle, Kidderminster
*Westminster, The Duke of, Eaton Hall, Chester
Wheeler, M. Alfred B., Manchester
Whitaker, Rev. Robert Nowell, M.A., Vicar of Whalley
Whitaker, W. W., St. Ann's Street, Manchester
Whitehead, James, M.D., Manchester
Whitelegge, Rev.William, M.A., Farnsfield Vicarage,
    Southwell, Notts
Whittaker, Rev. Robt., M.A., Leesfield, Oldham
Whitworth, Robert, Courtown House, Manchester
Wilkinson, Eason Matthew, M.D., Manchester
Wilkinson, T. R., The Grange, Didsbury
Wilkinson, T. T., Cheapside, Burnley
*Wilton, The Earl of, Heaton House, near Manchester
*Winmarleigh, The Lord, Winmarleigh, Lancashire
Wood, Richard Henry, F.S.A., Rugby, Hon. Secretary
Wood, Richard, Cornville House, Whalley Range
Woods, Sir Albert W., F.S.A., Garter King of Arms,
    College of Arms, London
Worsley, James E., Winwick Cottage, Winwick,
    Warrington

YATES, Edward, Liverpool

The Honorary Secretary requests that any change of address may be communicated to him
or to the Treasurer.

PRESENTATION OF THE PORTRAIT

OF

James Crossley, Esq., F.S.A.,

PRESIDENT OF THE CHETHAM SOCIETY,

TO THE CHETHAM LIBRARY,

4TH OCTOBER, 1875.

The following report of the proceedings of the Meeting at which this gratifying ceremonial took place, extracted from the Local Prints, is here inserted that it may be permanently preserved in the series of the Chetham Society's Publications.

——o——

AT the Easter meeting of the governors of the Chetham Hospital and Library, held in March of the present year, it was resolved that, in acknowledgment of the services for many years rendered to the library by Mr. JAMES CROSSLEY, F.S.A., chairman of the library committee, and in recognition of his valuable contributions to literature, his portrait should be painted and placed in the library. A committee was formed, with Mr. Hugh Birley, M.P., as chairman, Mr. Oliver Heywood as treasurer, and Mr. Henry Taylor as hon. secretary, to carry out the object, and a sufficient fund having been raised by subscription, Mr. John Hanson Walker of Kensington, London, was selected to execute a portrait, three-quarters life size. Mr. Crossley is represented in the portrait with a half-open volume in his hand, and the likeness is an excellent one. The portrait has been placed in the reading-room of Chetham's Library, and was formally presented

to the governors on the 4th October 1875, in the reading-room
of the library. Mr. Crossley was also presented with a beautifully
illuminated album, bound in morocco, which contained the resolution of the governors, the names of the committee, and the list
of subscribers to the portrait fund. There being a surplus over
the cost of Mr. Crossley's portrait, it had been devoted, with Mr.
Crossley's consent, to obtaining a portrait of Mr. THOMAS JONES,
B.A., F.S.A., the librarian, which has also been executed by Mr.
Walker, and hung in the library. This was also presented to the
governors on the same occasion.

At a MEETING of the Subscribers to the CROSSLEY MEMO-
RIAL FUND, held in the Reading-room of the Chetham Library,
on the 4th October 1875, Mr. HUGH BIRLEY, M.P., presided,
and among those present were the Rev. Canon Raines, the
Hon. Wilbraham Egerton, M.P., Rev. G. Heron, Chancellor
Christie, Rev. J. Brierley, Lieutenant-Colonel Sowler, Lieu-
tenant-Colonel Fishwick, Mr. Edward Joynson, Mr. R. Milne-
Redhead, Mr. R. H. Norreys, Mr. John Allen, Mr. Oliver
Heywood, Mr. H. T. Milne, Mr. George Thorley, Mr. J. E.
Bailey, Mr. G. W. Napier, Mr. Henry Ashworth, Dr. Ainsworth,
Mr. John Sudlow, and several other subscribers. It was an-
nounced that letters had been received from the Lord Bishop of
Manchester, Dr. Fleming, Rev. Canon H. M. Birch, Sir James
L. Bardsley, Mr. W. Harrison, F.S.A., Rev. John H. Marsden,
Mr. J. A. Bremner, Mr. Hugh Mason, Mr. Jas. Heywood, F.S.A.,
Mr. Tatton of Wythenshawe, and Mr. Richard Johnson, regrett-
ing their inability to be present on the occasion.

THE CHAIRMAN said that it would be difficult to suggest a
more appropriate gift to the Chetham Library, or, as he thought,
a more appropriate tribute of respect and esteem to Mr. Crossley
himself, than the portrait now offered to the governors. For a
period of fifty years, at least, Mr. Crossley had been devoted in
his attention to the Library ; for more than twenty years he had

been a governor of the College ; but he claimed their regard not only as a student and a governor, but also, and more especially, as one who, since that library was instituted by Humphrey Chetham, had drawn from it larger stores of learning, and had better known how to assimilate and apply that which he had learnt, than any other man. As President of the Chetham Society, and always the presiding genius, Mr. Crossley had illustrated with notes many of its valuable publications, and nothing that he had touched had he failed to adorn. Of the portrait itself he would only say that it did great credit to the artist, and that it satisfied, and more than satisfied, all the reasonable expectations of Mr. Crossley's friends. There had been ninety-four subscribers, and with his (Mr. Crossley's) entire approval, the surplus funds had been applied to the painting, by the same artist, of a portrait of Mr. Thomas Jones, who had been librarian at the College for upwards of thirty years. It only remained, now, formally to present the portrait to the governors, on whose behalf it would be accepted by the Rev. Canon Raines—himself one of the most able and painstaking antiquarians of the present age. Of Mr. Crossley, however, he had one more word to say. In one of his (Mr. Crossley's) pleasant notes to *Worthington's Diary*, in the Chetham series, they were told of a learned author who had many sons and daughters, and who, on the appearance of every addition to his family, was wont to issue a ponderous tome ; so that his friends and admirers were quite prepared, upon the appearance of one, to receive the announcement of the other. They had had too much reason to fear that Mr. Crossley would leave behind him neither books nor bairns, *nec libros nec liberos*. Now, however, if he (Mr. Birley) was not mistaken, yielding to the affectionate remonstrances of his friends, he had promised, or given something like a promise, to collect those scattered sibylline leaves which now lay buried in quarterly reviews and similar publications; and that very shortly they might hope to place upon those shelves "The Works of James Crossley." He (the Chairman) had great pleasure, on the part of the subscribers, in presenting this portrait, and would say to the governors, borrowing the sentiment of old Humphrey Chetham's motto, "Take what is now your own and keep good care of it."

The Rev. Canon RAINES said he had very great pleasure, on the part of the governors, in accepting the portrait so handsomely presented to the library, and felt sure that for many centuries to come it would remain an ornament to the institution, surrounded by the portraits of Humphrey Chetham, Dr. Whittaker, and other distinguished Lancashire men. He read the other day a letter addressed to George Chetham, the nephew and heir of the founder, by Mr. Lightbown of Manchester, which letter, though not dated, was clearly written shortly after the founder's death, and before the incorporation of the hospital in 1665. It referred to a portrait of the founder, and also to "a statue cut in marble," with his coat of arms, &c., which was to be "set over the college gate towards the school." He (Canon Raines) could not find either that the picture was provided for the College—unless the portrait over the reading-room mantelpiece was the one referred to—or that the marble statue was ever cut : for it was a sad reflection on human nature that individuals as well as nations, in these matters, were often "slowly wise and meanly just;" and buried merit was frequently left without the well-deserved picture, or the "storied urn or animated bust." A similar stigma would not, however, rest upon them as regarded the recognition of the valuable services rendered to the Chetham Library by their fellow-governor, Mr. Crossley, the most distinguished bibliophile in the north of England, and, he might add, the general favourite as the general friend. The governors would be delighted to have that memorial of Mr. Crossley, which, both as a likeness and as a work of art, was irreproachable.

The CHAIRMAN then handed to Mr. Crossley an album bearing the signatures of the subscribers, and stating that the memorial had been prepared in accordance with a resolution passed at the Easter meeting of the governors of the Chetham Hospital and

5

Library, "in acknowledgment of the services for many years rendered to the Chetham Library by Mr. James Crossley, chairman of the library committee, and in recognition of his valuable contributions to literature."

Mr. CROSSLEY (who was warmly cheered) said that he had in his library many rare and some unique books and MSS.; but certainly none that he should ever value in the same degree as the book, the *Album Amicorum*, which the chairman had placed in his hands. In it were contained the names of those kind and zealous friends to whom he owed—a debt he could never sufficiently acknowledge—the distinguished honour conferred upon him on that occasion. Distinctions such as this were gratifying at all periods of life. In early manhood they stimulated to further progress; in middle age they gave new interest in the past and new promise for the future; but he thought they were never so welcome and never so acceptable as at the close of life. They then showed that the veteran did not "lag superfluous on the stage." They showed that there was still a link between him and those around him, that the "coming generations," to use the phrase of a great poet, had not "pressed him down," and they helped to throw a cheering radiance on what remained of the little evening of his day. When he (Mr. Crossley) first came to Manchester in the year 1816, having left school, he had that interval which was generally conceded to young men before they entered upon a preparation for the active duties of life. He had a six months' furlough conceded to him, on that occasion, and it was left entirely with himself in what way he should employ the period. He set himself the task—which he had never since regretted—of going through the whole of the Latin poets, beginning with the fragments of Ennius and Lucilius, and ending with the last of the Poetæ Christiani. For that work the Chetham Library afforded every means in the shape of excellent editions and books that were necessary to enable him to go through it satisfactorily; and satisfactorily, certainly so far as his own feelings

went, he did go through it. During those six months, in the
year 1816, he might have been seen morning and afternoon at
the little bay window in that reading room. These were happy
mornings and pleasant afternoons, all undisturbed, except by the
chant of the boys to wonder-struck visitors—whose dreams must
have been haunted by "the crocodile, the alligator, and Oliver
Cromwell's sword"—and except when the hour had struck, and
the under librarian, grim Janitor! shaking his keys, admonished
the readers that they must go forth from that serene paradise of
books to the busy bustling world that surged beyond. If anyone
had said that the time would come, sixty years afterwards, when
standing in that room, certainly with as keen a relish for those
early pursuits as ever, and, he trusted, with as good a capacity,
mental and physical, for prosecuting them as ever; if anyone
had told him that he should look around and see the friendly
faces of so many respected citizens, and if they had said that on
that occasion he should likewise see his own portrait elevated
amongst the *dii tutelares* of that most charming of reading rooms,
in honoured companionship with the noble and beneficent founder,
with the great theological professor the opponent of Campian,
with the Dean of St. Paul's whose catechism was one of the
pillars of the English Church, with the martyr whose transcendent
merits he regretted to say had never found a memorial in
Manchester, and with one who was universally acknowledged
to be the first Greek scholar of his time, to say nothing of the
other worthies who were present on the walls, he should have
regarded the suggestion with infinite incredulity. But time, they
said, had its revenges ; and certainly it had its surprises too.
From that period, though no longer a regular student there, it had
been one of his great delights to come whenever an opportunity
presented itself, and to investigate at the fountain head the many
subjects and questions which have interest to a literary man.
He had never left that room without finding his mind freshened
and invigorated by contact and communion with those inestimable
old folios. In the year 1843, he became bound by an additional

tic to that library, namely, the establishment of the Chetham Society, whose first meeting took place, through the kindness of Mr. Hulton, then librarian, in that room. From the circumstance of their meeting there the society took its name, and therefore it might be considered to be an offshoot of the library ; and when the fact was considered that it had now lasted for thirty-two years, and that it had produced nearly 100 volumes, he thought it would be admitted that it had been a very vigorous offshoot of the parent tree. Another society which had been started, and of which he had also the honour to be president, had likewise held its meetings there — the Spenser Society — whose object was to reproduce the poetical literature of the time of Elizabeth and the two monarchs who succeeded her ; and certainly its proceedings could scarcely have been commenced with greater propriety anywhere than in the rooms of that building, where it was known the worthies of the time of Elizabeth were entertained, and where the shadows of some great men, Sir Henry Saville, Sir Walter Raleigh, and others, might almost seem by fancy's eye, in the dim evenings, to flit along the walls in search of their friend the wizard warden. Twenty years ago—an additional tie to the institution—he became one of the governors of the Hospital and Library ; and he might say that, in so doing, he became associated with as conscientious and as honourable a body of men as ever were called upon to fulfil the duties of a public trust. He felt a natural and deep interest in the library, which had extended from 18,000 to close upon 40,000 volumes; and had had the great satisfaction of meeting, as librarian, one who seemed designed by nature for the place, and whose whole soul was in his work. He mentioned these matters to show the various points of interest which had connected him with the institution for so long a period. So much had it become an intellectual necessary of life to him that he should never, he trusted, be separated from it. He might almost say, *Sit anima mea cum Bibliothecâ Chethamensi*. He trusted that visitors to that place, seeing his portrait, would remember him as one who, though he might not, perhaps, boast of any high degree of literary merit in the productions which had been so flatteringly referred to, yet in point of ardent love and zeal for books and libraries, and for good literature in its fullest measure and largest extent, would concede to no man living. In conclusion, he expressed a hope that that admirable institution—the monument of such charity— would ever be kept inviolate. He trusted that the hospital and library, so harmoniously brought together by the founder, which represented in so high a degree the whole scope and extent of his bounty, would never be separated. He was sure the people of Manchester ought to consider that institution as the apple of their eye. Every traveller from every part of the civilised world who came to Manchester, when he saw that building, had something to say in its favour. A friend of his, Mr. Axon, placed in his hands the other day a book by Dr. Collyer of Chicago, which contained a long panegyric on Humphrey Chetham and the institution which he founded. He trusted that it would always remain there, and that the library would go on extending till it had reached proportions of which neither Mr. Jones (the librarian) nor himself had the slightest conception. (Mr. Crossley then sat down amidst great cheering.)

The CHAIRMAN then presented to the governors of the College the portrait of Mr. Jones, which he trusted would be accepted as a worthy tribute to that gentleman's merits and character.

The Rev. Canon RAINES, on the part of the governors, accepted the portrait, and observed that all that had been said in praise of the librarian by Mr. Crossley and by the chairman was well deserved.

A vote of thanks to the chairman concluded the meeting.